Berry Picking Time

Story Keeper Series
Book 3

Dave and Pat Sargent (*left*) are longtime residents of Prairie Grove, Arkansas. Dave, a fourth-generation dairy farmer, began writing in early December 1990. Pat, a former teacher, began writing in the fourth grade. They enjoy the outdoors and have a real love for animals.

Sue Rogers (*right*) returned to her beloved Mississippi after retirement. She shared books with children for more than thirty years. These stories fulfill a dream of writing books—to continue the sharing.

Berry Picking Time

Story Keeper Series
Book 3

By Dave and Pat Sargent
and Sue Rogers

Beyond "The End"
By Sue Rogers

Illustrated by Jane Lenoir

Ozark Publishing, Inc.
P.O. Box 228
Prairie Grove, AR 72753

Cataloging-in-Publication Data

Sargent, Dave, 1941–
    Berry picking time / by Dave and
Pat Sargent and Sue Rogers ; illustrated by
Jane Lenoir.—Prairie Grove, AR : Ozark
Publishing, c2004.
    p. cm. (Story keeper series ; 3)

    "Be brave"—Cover.
    SUMMARY: Nanto has a fierce desire to
become an Apache warrior. Will he be brave
enough when his chance comes?
    ISBN 1-56763-907-0 (hc)
           1-56763-908-9 (pbk)

    1. Indians of North America—Juvenile
fiction. 2. Apache Indians—Juvenile fiction.
[1. Native Americans—United States—Fiction.
2. Apache Indians—Fiction.] I. Sargent,
Pat, 1936– II. Rogers, Sue, 1933– III. Lenoir,
Jane, 1950– ill. IV. Title. V. Series.

    PZ7.S243Be 2004
    [Fic]—dc21   2003090090

Printed in the United States of America

iv

Inspired by
the way the American Indian
families cherish their children.

Dedicated to
all children
"warmed by the sun,
rocked by the winds,
and sheltered by the trees."

Foreword

Little Nanto had been taught the legends of his Apache people, taught by his mother of the sun and sky, the moon and stars, the clouds and storms, taught to kneel and pray to Usen for strength, health, wisdom, and protection. He would soon become old enough to be considered a youth, and he had a fierce desire to become an Apache warrior.

Contents

If you would like to have the authors of the Story Keeper Series visit your school, free of charge, just call us at 1-800-321-5671 or 1-800-960-3876.

One

Berries for the Winter

Every berry near the tepee camp had been gathered and dried. Mother's family needed many berries for the winter. Dried berries were mashed and used to make pemmican for our warriors. They packed it in leather bags and tied the bags to their belts. It took only a small amount of this to satisfy their hunger when they traveled far from the stew pots that bubble in their wickiups. Extra pemmican was stored for the family.

Game could be scarce during the long cold winter. If we found enough fresh berries, Mother might crush and mix them with water and honey to make a special drink for us.

My mother decided that after a sleep, all the women and children would go in a party to hunt berries. In two moons I would be considered a youth. I had a fierce desire to become a warrior.

"Picking berries will not train me to be a great warrior," I thought. "But running will." I knew we were going far from camp because Mother said we would take ponies. I would run ahead to scout for berries. That would mean we could pick more berries in less time. The run would make me stronger. The run would increase my speed and strength.

"Nanto, be sure the baskets will not slip on my pony once they are filled with berries," cautioned my mother.

"Yes, Mother," I said.

My grandmother had woven all the baskets. Like a warm summer breeze, memories of her strong hands working with the willow whiffed through my mind. I heard her laugh again when I pinched one of the cochineal bugs we had gathered. My fingers turned red and so did the tip of my nose where the juice squirted. Now I saw the red dye in the baskets.

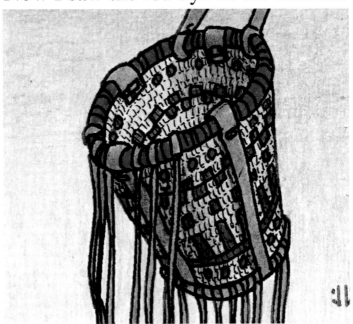

My grandmother told me many stories of my grandfather as she worked on the designs. She told of my father's bravery when he was a young warrior. My grandmother was the one who taught me the traditions of our people.

"Once another old grandmother got annoyed with a deer," her next story began. "The deer had followed a young Apache boy out from the underworld with the other animals. The old grandmother lived in a brush lodge. The deer was hungry. It ate some of her lodge covering. The old grandmother snatched a stick from the fire and struck the deer's nose. The white ash stuck there on its nose. It left a white mark. The white mark can still be seen on the nose of deer today."

"Hereafter, you shall avoid all mankind," the old grandmother said. "Your nose will tell you when you are too close to them."

"Today it is mostly at night when deer appear," continued my grandmother. "Not too close. They remember the old grandmother told them to be guided by their noses."

The baskets were completed,
but never the stories.

Two

Cho-ko-le Is Lost

Morning dew still glistened on the grass. The wet footprints where I had run pointed toward the berries. Our party followed them. Just when the sun became warm on our backs and the dew was gone, we arrived.

"You saved us much searching time by running ahead, my son," said my mother. "I am pleased with your wise thinking. Warriors must have sharp minds as well as sharp eyes."

My mother was the wise one. She understood. She knew how much I wanted to be a great warrior.

Plunk, plunk! As the baskets began to fill, laughter and talk filled the air. Cradleboards hung from tree limbs. They swung sleeping babies back and forth in the wind.

Young children played their favorite game of hide-and-seek. They played at chasing imaginary animals. Some popped a few ripe berries into their mouths. Older children, like me, were busy picking red berries. Everyone was happy that the berry pickings were so good.

My mother and I worked our way to a grove of tall pine trees. We found many more berry bushes. There would be plenty of berries for the winter now. They were sweet and juicy. My mother smiled when she saw the stain on my lips!

"Tonight we will have berry cakes," my mother said.

A woman named Cho-ko-le had gotten lost from our party. She could no longer see our people or hear their happy voices. Both baskets on her pony were full, so she swung up onto his back and began to look for the others. Where could they be?

She had been so busy that she got too far away from the others. She would follow her pony's tracks. That should take her back. She rode through a thicket in search of her friends. Her little dog was following. She was so intent on watching for her pony's tracks that she forgot to look around her. She forgot to listen for sounds of danger. All of a sudden a grizzly bear rose in her path and attacked the pony. The woman jumped off. The pony escaped, but the bear attacked Cho-ko-le.

Apache girls always carried a knife in their knee-high moccasins. Cho-ko-le quickly drew out her knife. She swung at the grizzly bear with her knife. Swish! Swish! Swish!

Cho-ko-le fought for her life. Her little dog snapped at the bear's heels. This distracted the bear. He was not used to having his heels nipped with sharp little teeth.

This gave Cho-ko-le time to jump out of the bear's reach. The bear was not quick, but he was big. He had long legs and could reach way out. Finally the grizzly bear struck Cho-ko-le over the head. He made deep tears in her scalp and knocked her to the ground.

Cho-ko-le struggled to remain conscious. She was able to strike the bear four good licks with her knife. The grizzly bear retreated. After the bear was gone, Cho-ko-le replaced her torn scalp. She bound it up as best she could. She became very sick and had to lie down. Her little dog lay beside her.

Three

Alone and Wounded

The gathering party was happy about how many berries we had found. Mothers strapped the cradle-boards on their backs. Children were called together. Ties holding the full berry baskets were checked.

We believe that all of creation has a spirit. My mother expressed our gratitude to the spirits of the berries. The ponies were moving very slowly with their heavy loads. Thoughts turned to the empty wicki-ups waiting for us. In all the excite-ment, no one noticed that Cho-ko-le

19

was not with us when we went back to the camp.

That night Cho-ko-le's pony came into camp with his load of berries, but with no rider.

The women, the children, and the warriors searched for Cho-ko-le all the next day. They did not find her. After a sleep, they would return to the new berry patch and look again. This time they would take her pony. Maybe he would lead them to the lost woman.

Long before smoke from the revived morning fire began to curl out of my father's wickiup the next day, my pony and I were racing toward the forest. We were soon near the thick underbrush and tall pine trees where we had last seen Cho-ko-le. The sun had not yet reached the ground below the branches of the trees. Long shadows stretched along the earth. The shadows seemed to be reaching for anyone who came near. There was no warmth.

I felt in the pouch that was tied to my waist. The flat stone that my grandmother had painted with a magic design was there.

"The magic will keep you safe," she had said. A crow flew overhead. I entered the forest.

With no sounds but the wind whispering through the tall pines, I listened. Scents drifted from the earth and trees. I smelled. The sun was brighter. I could see. Then a feeling of the presence of another body tickled down my spine. There are big bears in this forest, I recalled. I drew my bow and arrow, ready!

But if it was a bear, the bow and arrow might not be enough. My spear with the sharp bone would be better. I pulled it from the leather sheath. I gripped it, held it high.

My little pony slowly moved around a thicket of berry bushes. I was hardly breathing. Then I saw a movement beneath a pine just ahead, such a tiny movement—not like a charging bear. It was Cho-ko-le! She was hurt!

I was still a boy, but lifting heavy loads for my mother had made my arms strong. My legs were solid and sturdy from running.

I picked Cho-ko-le up in my arms and laid her across my shoulder. Holding her with one arm, I swung up onto my pony.

I sat the injured woman on my pony's back so that my body could brace her and cradle her head.

Cho-ko-le was very brave. She was quiet. She never made a sound.

We were barely out of the forest when we met the search party returning to look for Cho-ko-le. They helped carry her home. The medicine men in our camp put oak bark on her wounds. They knew what herbs to use for medicine. They knew how to prepare them and how to use them.

Under their careful treatment, all of Cho-ko-le's wounds healed.

27

Finding Cho-ko-le by myself made the warriors think that I might be brave enough to become one of them. "In two moons when you become a youth, would you like to go on the next warpath with us, Nanto?" they invited.

This was the first of four tests. The beginning of my life-dream!

"You will be ready, my son," said my mother.

"Nanto, they will find you both industrious and quick. You will never speak out of order. You will be discreet in all things. Your courage in battle will be admired. Hardships will not cause you to complain. They will find no color of cowardice, or weakness of any kind," my father said. "You will meet all your tests courageously. You will prove that you are a stranger to fear," he said proudly. "Then, my son, you will surely be admitted to the council of the warriors."

All this made me very happy. Best of all, my father smiled.

And then, my mother whispered softly, "Sheth she~n zho~n." ("I love you" in the Apache language.)

Four

Apache Facts

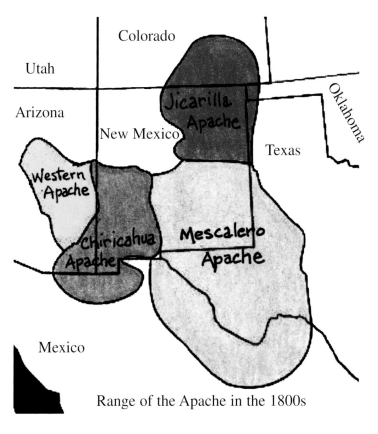

Range of the Apache in the 1800s

Teepee (Tipi): Eastern Apache in the southern plains lived in teepees.

Wickiup: Western and mountain Apaches lived in wickiups.

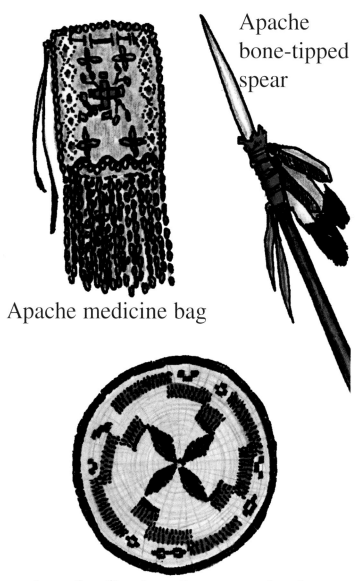

Apache bone-tipped spear

Apache medicine bag

Apache flat bowl, woven basket

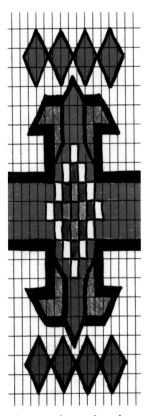

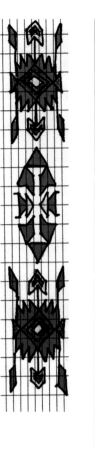

Apache designs
(Left to Right):
  Shoulder band
  Choker
  Belt

Buffalo   Church   Hand

Horse   Indian and dog   Indian and pony

Longhorn   Cow   Cowboy

Man with rifle   Sun   White man

Pictographs from Palo Duro Canyon, and Big Bend, in Texas

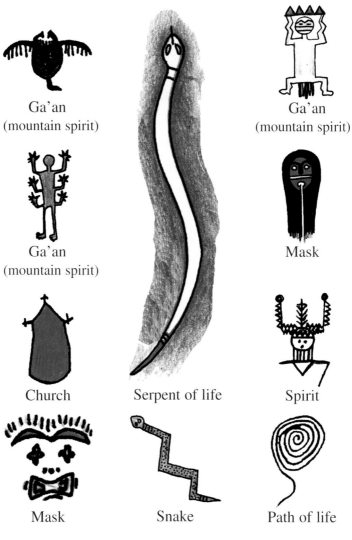

Ga'an
(mountain spirit)

Ga'an
(mountain spirit)

Ga'an
(mountain spirit)

Mask

Church

Serpent of life

Spirit

Mask

Snake

Path of life

Pictographs from Apache territories,
all believed to be Apache

36

Beyond "The End"

● Geronimo once said, "I was born on the prairies where the wind blew free and there was nothing to break the light of the sun. I was born where there were no enclosures." What did this mean to a youth who had been taught the legends of his people, taught by his mother of the sun and sky, the moon and stars, the clouds and storms? Write a poem expressing Geronimo's feelings.

CURRICULUM CONNECTIONS

● To which cultural group did the Apache tribe belong? What present-day states of the United States were their lands in before the Europeans came?

● Where do the Apaches live today? Do Apache boys dream of becoming fierce warriors today? Make a list of five ways life has changed for a young Apache boy. Make a list of five ways life has changed for a young girl.

● Do you think Nanto was brave? Why? Are you brave? Why?

● It was said that an Apache warrior could run 50 miles without stopping and travel more swiftly than a troop of mounted soldiers. If a warrior needed to run 150 miles, with short rests every 50 miles, how many rest stops would he need to make?

● What was pemmican? How did Native Americans make it? See <www.smokylake.com/history/native/pemmican.htm>.

● Although the Apaches did not have a number system, numbers were an important part of their religious beliefs. An Apache prayed to his gods at least once every four days, and if possible, every day, four times a day. Apache medicine men used four in their remedies. They might use four roots of one herb or one root each of four herbs.

● Think about all the ways you use numbers in your life. How would you manage without numbers?

THE ARTS

● Read one of the Apache legends, *Origin of Fire*, at <http://impurplehawk.com/folklore2.html>. Draw pictures to illustrate this legend.

GATHERING INFORMATION

● Nanto and his people gathered much of the food that they ate. They gathered berries, nuts, and roots that grew wild in nature.

● When you need information for a report or a class project, you "gather" facts from many different sources. Most of the information you need is found in books in your school library media center. Can you tell what kind of information you will find in these books (references)?

      Dictionary
      Encyclopedia
      Atlas
      Almanac

THE BEST I CAN BE

● To understand Native Americans, we must be able to grasp their belief that we all belong to and are protectors of the Earth. Just as Nanto's footprints in the dew-covered grass showed the path he had taken to the berries, your "ecological footprints" show your path and measure its impact on the Earth's resources. Sit in the warm sunshine and think about what you can do to protect the earth.